The Diary

of

Robin's Toys

Ken and Angie Lake

1

Geraldo the Giraffe

Published by Sweet Cherry Publishing Limited
53 St. Stephens Road,
Leicester, LE2 1GH
United Kingdom

First Published in the UK in 2013

ISBN: 978-1-78226-022-6

Title: Geraldo the Giraffe - The Diaries of Robin's Toys

Printed and Bound By Nutech Print Services, India

4

Every Toy Has a Story to Tell

Have you ever seen an old toy perhaps in a cupboard, or in the attic or loft? Have you ever seen how sad they look at car boot sales, unwanted and unloved? Well, look at them closely, because every toy has a story to tell, and the older, the more decrepit, the more scruffy, the more tatty the toy is, the more interesting its story could be. Here are just a few of those toys and their stories.

18th March, 09.25

It was a cloudy Sunday morning, and as Robin looked down the street and waited for Grandad, he thought about his week at school.

He hated to see other children being bullied. But there was one little girl called Caroline; actually, she wasn't that little...

You see, Caroline's mum always gave her chips and

chocolate and sweets and doughnuts, and not much else.

Poor Caroline had no idea what an apple or a tomato even looked like. She never ate any fruit or vegetables. In fact, she had no proper healthy food at all.

She had trouble keeping up in sports, and when they went swimming she refused to come out of the changing rooms.

She just didn't feel good about herself, and some of the children picked on her and called her names. Caroline was - even though Robin had been told not to use the word - a bit fat!

And it was very obvious to him and everybody else that Caroline's mum was quite, err... big as well.

Poor Caroline didn't have any real friends, but she pretended not to care about being...well, let's just say... overweight.

But as Robin watched her walking around the playground on her own, he felt really sorry for her.

Then, as the clouds started to clear and the sun peeped through, there was Grandad's little red car.

Beep, beep!

"Come on, Robin."

Beep, beep!

And off they went to the car boot sale.

Grandad gave Robin 50 pence and they walked round and round the stalls. It was a nice day, even though it was still a bit cloudy, and there were lots of happy people chatting and laughing.

Some of them had bulging bags, while others struggled to carry bits of furniture or books. Two women were carrying an old moose head with huge horns, which kept poking people as they tried to pass them.

"Grandad, you know, I feel really sorry for this poor little girl at school."

"Oh really, Robin, why is that?"

"The problem is, everyone makes fun of her because she is ... different."

"What do you mean, Robin?"

"Well, I am not really supposed to say this, so please don't tell anyone that I did, but

Caroline is, well ... heavier than the other children, and she gets called names at school. I know it's not her fault, but her mum doesn't know how to cook and she keeps giving her chips and doughnuts and fatty foods. Am I allowed to say fatty foods, Grandad?"

"Oh yes, Robin, I am sure you are allowed to say that."

"I would really like to help her, but I don't know what to do about it."

"Okay, Robin, let's think about it this morning while we wander around the car boot sale."

Just in front of them a
smiley lady with curly hair and
old-fashioned glasses was
carrying a pink lampshade;
you know, the sort with tassels
around the bottom.

Her husband grabbed it and put it on his head. Then he did a silly walk, and lots of people laughed.

Just behind her was a skinny man with an itchy beard and spots. He looked like an Arthur, but it was difficult to tell if he really was an Arthur. Anyway, he was wearing one of those old shirts; you know, the sort with a big flap at the back. Robin had no idea what that was for, but the man seemed quite proud that it was hanging out from under his jacket.

Anyway, Arthur was swinging a budgie's cage; it was painted blue, with bits of rust here and there. But it was empty.

A breeze started to blow
away what was left of the
clouds, and then the sun shone
and brightened up all of the
stalls.

That was the moment Robin saw him sitting proudly at the front of Albert All-Sorts' stall.

"Grandad ... Grandad, that's the first giraffe I have seen at the car boot sale. May I buy him, please?"

Grandad had the magical power to speak to toys, so he said, "Let me have a quick chat with him first to see if he has had an interesting life."

Grandad cast his secret spell and seemed to go into a trance.

"Oh yes, Robin, he may be just what you need. You had better ask the man how much he would like for him."

"Err, excuse me, Mr All-Sorts, how much is that toy giraffe?"

"Well, young man, this is an extra-special gourmet giraffe."

"I am sorry, I don't know what a gourmet is."

"Gourmet is a French word for someone who is supposed to know a lot about food, but the word can also be used for someone who eats a lot. So now you know that, how much do you

think Geraldo the Gourmet
Giraffe is really worth?"

"I am not sure how much he is worth, but I only have 50 pence. Is that enough?"

"I really wanted a pound, but you look like a nice boy. Go on then, he is yours for 50 pence. Shall I put him in a bag for you? And remember, don't feed him too much."

The man laughed and waved goodbye to Geraldo.

"Do you like your gourmet giraffe?" Grandad asked.

"Oh, he's very nice, and I can't wait to hear his story. I wonder what he has done in his life."

After a bit more wandering
around they took Geraldo home,

put him on the kitchen table and
Grandad cast his magic spell...

"Little toy, hear this rhyme,
Let it take you back in time,
Tales of sadness or of glory,
Little toy, reveal your story."

The toy giraffe began to shake a little and gradually started to move his long neck. He slowly opened one eye, then the other... Suddenly, his little face came alive and he looked around, as if someone had just woken him up from a long sleep.

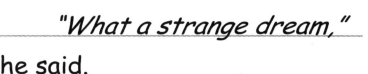

"*What a strange dream,*" he said.

"Hello, Geraldo," said Robin.

"Oh, hello, young man," the giraffe replied. *"I'm not too sure where I am."*

"Don't worry," said Robin. "Grandad and I woke you. We know that you are called Geraldo and were told that you were a gourmet. We thought you looked very interesting and wanted to know a bit more about you."

"Oh, thank you, young man.
So, you want to know the story
of my life. Well, where should
I start?"

"Giraffes live in herds on the plains of Africa, where we wander around eating the leaves from trees; that is our natural food.

"Over many, many years we have developed very long necks, so that we can easily reach the leaves at the tops of the trees which other animals can't.

"Now, Robin, have you ever looked closely at a giraffe?"

"Err actually, Geraldo, no, I haven't."

" *Well go on then; now that you have one in front of you, have a good look at me.*

" *"You will see that I have long, thin legs and the longest neck of any animal on Earth. And I am covered in pretty brown spots. But having a neck which is so long can cause some very serious problems.*

"Have you ever tried to buy a scarf for your favourite giraffe?

"Don't even bother to try; they don't make scarves that long! Even Nelly Knitwear would have problems knitting a scarf for a giraffe.

"Then of course there is the old joke about the giraffe's sore throat going a long way down, but sore throats are not so funny for a giraffe. Can you imagine how much throat medicine it takes to make us feel better?

"But the main problem we have, and not many people realise this, is that we are always feeling hungry.

"This is because it takes so long for our food to travel from our mouths to our tummies.

It's such a long way down, that by the time breakfast has got there, I have already had my mid-morning snack, followed by lunch and another mid-meal snack, and then I am thinking about what to have for dinner.

"That's why food is very important for giraffes.

"And can you imagine what it's like wandering around the African plains and standing on tiptoes all day long, just to nibble a few leaves? Well, I can tell you, it's not great. My legs used to ache and my neck got sore.

"And that's not all, Robin. Although I had been brought up on leaves, I was beginning to find them a bit ordinary. What I really wanted to try was all the foods which people eat.

"But the only way I could think of to do this was for me to learn to cook.

"Unfortunately, I had no idea about cooking; I never learned about it at giraffe school and it was something that very few *giraffes ever did. I mean, when did you last see a famous giraffe chef on TV?*

"*Luckily there was a closing down sale at a local bookshop, so I went along and bought myself a cookery book called*

Basic Cookery for Giraffes.

"It had lots of nice colour pictures, lots of easy explanations about proper cooking and some very interesting. recipes. I couldn't wait to get home and try some of them out.

I opened up page one: Scrambled Eggs.

And I read it slowly. Take 2 eggs, remove their shells and put the eggs in a bowl.

"But I never did follow instructions very well and had already cracked 12 eggs, not 2 as it said in the book.

"A little voice in my head was saying: Err, it will probably be easier if you have the bowl ready first! But I did manage to scoop up the eggs, and then I put most of them into the bowl.

    "Then the recipe said: Put in some salt (no, just a pinch, not the whole pot) and a sprinkle of pepper. Make sure that the lid is screwed on before you shake the pepper !

"But it was too late...
Hachoo! Hachoo! Yes, that's
when I learned that pepper
really does make you sneeze!

"So I read the next bit: *Now mix it up with a fork. I soon found out that using the pointed end is much easier. Then it said: put some butter in a pan and heat it gently.*

"What was that burning smell? *I read the next instruction: Put the mixture into the warm pan and cook for a few minutes. As soon as it's cooked, eat it.* Well, I didn't need any instructions on eating it.

"It tasted fantastic, and
I couldn't wait to try the next
recipe: Cheese and Onion Tart.

"It said: Chop the onion. Oh
alright, if you can't chop it, then

crush it. Alright, stand on it and jump up and down if you really have to.

"Then chop up some cheese; yes, yes, go on, stand on that as well if you must.

"Make some pastry; yes, I agree it's much quicker to buy it ready-made. Put the cheese and onion in the pastry and cook it until it's done.

51

"Waiting was the worst bit, as I was very hungry. So as soon as it was cooked and cool I bent my long neck down and attacked it with my mouth. I have to tell you, the flavour was just wonderful.

"Then, after I had eaten it, I made the next recipe in the book: Cottage Pie.

"At first I did wonder about the name, but the little voice in my head said: No, Geraldo, let's be sensible, nobody really eats cottages.

"I had never been very sure about the measures, and I knew that cottages were big; well, that was my excuse anyway. So I stuck to my idea of bigger is better and made a huge one.

"I had the idea of inviting all my friends around to eat it with me. But it didn't quite work out that way, because the cottage pie was so tasty that I had to eat it all to check it was delicious all the way through.

"After all those years of wandering around nibbling leaves, I was eating real people food at last!

"It was so fantastic that I had a big, big smile on my face as I turned the page and looked at the next delicious recipe. It was a great experience for me to taste so many different flavours.

"I just couldn't wait to make the next recipe, which was a Curry. It wasn't too difficult to cook, but I was still a bit confused about tablespoons, teaspoons, cups and fluid ounces and litre measures. I got them wrong and used the big measure for everything.

"So what should have been a mild curry turned out to be the hottest thing I had ever tasted, but it was not a problem.

"I had never experienced anything like it before and I thought the flavour was amazing.

"I thought I was in heaven with all those different foods. But as the scrambled eggs hadn't got all the way to my tummy yet, I was still very hungry.

"The next recipe was Shepherd's Pie, and I was confused about the name again.

"I thought to myself, it can't be made with real shepherds, can it? But the little voice in my head said: Don't be silly, Geraldo, it's probably made by shepherds, or more likely for shepherds.

"Again, I doubled all the ingredients and made a huge one. It wasn't difficult to make and it was absolutely delicious.

"I had soon worked my way through the main part of the cookbook , and then came to the section on desserts, or puddings as they are sometimes called. These looked irresistible, so I read on.

"A recipe for Trifle, now that sounded great. I mixed three different-coloured jellies, although I knew that one would have been enough. Then I put in two sponges where I should have used one.

"I made a big pan of custard to put on the top, and then as soon as it was set I covered it in whipped cream. Then, to make it look really pretty, I sprinkled on lots and lots of flaked chocolate. Wow! I had created a wobbly monster.

"I used the same excuse again about sharing it with my friends, but of course, after a few minutes, there was nothing left to share. I had eaten the whole lot!

"Then I slowly turned the pages and made every other dessert in the book, and ate the whole lot. I realised that I was being much more than a Gourmet Giraffe; I was being a Greedy Gourmet Giraffe.

"By this time I was getting a message from the little voice in my tummy: It's getting really full down here; I hope there isn't any more food on the way down!

"But there was, lots and lots of it! After a while I began to feel a bit poorly; in fact, I soon felt really sick, but when you have such a long neck, being sick is not an option.

"I decided to go outside for some air, but then I got a message from the little voice in my legs: We are afraid we can't touch the ground, so, Geraldo, you are going nowhere.

"I looked down and saw that my tummy was so full and big that my legs were quite a long way off the ground; they were just dangling, and useless.

"It was National Giraffe Day, and lots of my friends came round to see me, but I was stuck and couldn't join in with the fun and games.

"I remember spending several hours stranded, like a beached whale. My friends thought it was very funny and just laughed at me.

"I felt very sorry for myself and very, very silly. The next day I managed to waddle as far as the nearest tree. But it took a long, long time before my tummy was anywhere near back to normal, and I could join the rest of my friends in the giraffe herd.

"Even when I did join them, they still teased me about the time when I ate too much, and my tummy was so big that my legs couldn't reach the ground. But at least I had learned why giraffes are designed only to nibble leaves.

"I had learned a valuable lesson and never wanted to eat so much again. I really wanted to be a happy and healthy giraffe, so I approached a nearby safari park and made friends with Rachel, one of the *keepers. She took me in and made sure I got a proper healthy diet, with lots of fresh food and plenty of exercise.*

"I was scared of getting ill again and didn't want to eat anything but leaves, but Rachel taught me that it's okay to try new things and to have a bit of everything in your diet, as long as you don't eat too much of the wrong things and you get plenty of exercise.

"I came back with her to a zoo in England, but when it closed down I went from home to home until I ended up at the car boot sale."

All through the story
Robin had been thinking about
Caroline. She was being laughed
at just like Geraldo.

On Monday morning he watched her at school. She didn't join in with any of the games, and when the girls' hockey teams were picked, she wasn't included. It was the same story when the girls' netball team was chosen; Caroline was left out.

She pretended she didn't care, but Robin could see that she was hurting on the inside and he thought he saw a little tear trickle down her cheek.

Children can be so cruel to anyone who is a bit different. Going home on the school bus she always sat at the front on her own. Some of the children pretended that she smelled bad, but that just wasn't true.

Robin was quite upset and wondered how Caroline felt about it. It must have been awful for her to be bullied and laughed at all the time.

How would the bullies feel if they were being picked on? He had to try to do something, but what?

When he got home he telephoned Grandad and they had a long chat about it.

"Well, Grandad, what do you think I should do to help poor Caroline?"

"It seems to me that Caroline is going through the same problems as Geraldo the

Giraffe. All of his friends laughed at him when he was different too."

"Yes, Grandad, you are right there. Do you think it will help if Caroline hears Geraldo's story?"

"I don't think it can do any harm. What do you think?"

"Yes, Grandad, I think you are right about this, but then you seem to be right about everything."

"Well, Robin, that's just one of the advantages of being old, although there aren't very many. But I have seen a lot more things in my long life, and learning from them is very important. It's so easy to think that you know everything, but nobody does, so keep listening and learning; it's an important lesson."

The next day after school, Robin invited Caroline round to his house for tea and to meet Geraldo. She was so excited that somebody actually wanted to be friends with her that she said, "Yes please," straight away.

Robin's mum had made a nice salad with fresh tomatoes and cucumber from the greenhouse, and fresh lettuce from the garden. They had proper free-range hard-boiled eggs from the farm just up the road and some wonderful new potatoes.

It was all so fresh and so healthy!

She had also made a fruit
salad, again with wonderful
fresh ingredients like
strawberries and apples, many
of them from their own garden.

Caroline didn't know what to say. At first she didn't think that she would like proper food; she had never had anything like it before and all the flavours were so different. But she loved it, absolutely loved it! And she said so.

Robin's mum was very pleased, because there is nothing worse than making a meal for somebody who won't eat it. Caroline went home a much happier girl than when she arrived, and she told her mum all about the fantastic experience.

The next morning Robin took Geraldo into school and gave him to Caroline. She was so pleased! And when she took him home he told her his story, about how eating too much of the wrong food will make you... Oh, you know, that word which

we all know but are not supposed
to use!

After hearing Geraldo's
story, Caroline understood. It
was very hard for her to start
being healthy, but Geraldo was
there every step of the way.
They had healthy tea parties
with her other toys, and he
went with her on outdoor

adventures like bike rides and walks in the countryside.

So, with lots of support from Geraldo and her mum and dad, Caroline eventually became a happy, healthy girl.

She was delighted when she was picked for both the netball team and the hockey team. And as for the bullies?

Well, with friends like Geraldo and Robin, who cared what they thought!